SAILOR TAYLOR SETS SAIL

By David F. Marx
Illustrated by Lynn Avril-Cravath

BARRON'S

Table of Contents

Illustration on page 21 by Carol Stutz; Illustrations on pages 22–23 by Deborah Gross

All inquiries should be addressed to:
Barron's Educational Series, Inc.
250 Wireless Boulevard
Hauppauge, New York 11788
www.barronseduc.com

Library of Congress Catalog Card No.: 2006028818

ISBN-13: 978-0-7641-3720-4
ISBN-10: 0-7641-3720-4

Library of Congress Cataloging-in-Publication Data
Marx, David F.
    Sailor Taylor sets sail / by David F. Marx.
        p. cm. — (Reader's clubhouse)
    ISBN-13: 978-0-7641-3720-4
    ISBN-10: 0-7641-3720-4
    1. Reading—Phonetic method. 2. Readers (Primary)   I. Title.

LB1573.3.M33 2007
372.46'5—dc22

                                                                2006028818

PRINTED IN CHINA
9 8 7 6 5 4 3 2 1

Dear Parent and Educator,

Welcome to the Barron's Reader's Clubhouse, a series of books that provide a phonics approach to reading.

Phonics is the relationship between letters and sounds. It is a system that teaches children that letters have specific sounds. Level 1 books introduce the short-vowel sounds. Level 2 books progress to the long-vowel sounds. Level 3 books then go on to vowel combinations and words ending in "y." This progression matches how phonics is taught in many classrooms.

Sailor Taylor Sets Sail introduces the "ai" and "ay" vowel combination sound. Simple words with these vowel combinations are called **decodable words.** The child knows how to sound out these words because he or she has learned the sound they include. This story also contains **high-frequency words.** These are common, everyday words that the child learns to read by sight. High-frequency words help ensure fluency and comprehension. **Challenging words** go a little beyond the reading level. The child may need help from an adult to understand these words. All words are listed by their category on page 24.

Here are some coaching and prompting statements you can use to help a young reader read *Sailor Taylor Sets Sail:*

- **On page 4, "Spain" is a decodable word. Point to the word and say:**

  Read this word. How did you know the word? What sounds did it make?

  Note: There are many opportunities to repeat the above instruction throughout the book.

- **On page 9, "birthday" is a challenging word. Point to the word and say:**

  Read this word. Sound out the word. How did you know the word? What helped you?

You'll find more coaching ideas on the Reader's Clubhouse Web site: *www.barronsclubhouse.com.* Reader's Clubhouse is designed to teach and reinforce reading skills in a fun way. We hope you enjoy helping children discover their love of reading!

Sincerely,

Nancy Harris

Nancy Harris
Reading Consultant

On Monday, Sailor Taylor was going to sail to Spain. Along came her friend, Ray Cain.

They were all set to go. But Ray Cain said, Wait! We did not bring the mail. Go back and get the mail for Spain.

On Tuesday, Sailor Taylor was
going to sail to Spain. She was
all set to go.

But Ray Cain said, Wait! We
need a bigger crew. And they
will need money to get paid.

On Wednesday, Sailor Taylor
was going to sail to Spain. She
was all set to go.

But Ray Cain said, Wait! My
birthday is soon. What will we
play on my day?

On Thursday, Sailor Taylor was going to sail to Spain. She was all set to go.

But Ray Cain said, Wait! What
will we eat? We must fish for
our food with some bait.

On Friday, Sailor Taylor was
going to sail to Spain. She was
all set to go.

But Ray Cain said, Wait! Our
ship is too plain. We must go
back for some paint.

On Saturday, Sailor Taylor was
going to sail to Spain. She was
all set to go.

But Ray Cain said, Wait! Our
sail has a rip. We must bring
along a tailor.

On Sunday, Sailor Taylor was
going to sail to Spain. They
were all set to go. They all said,
Ray! Is there another thing you
want to say?

No, said Ray Cain. Please, let us go. I want us to sail to Spain.

Then came the rain. Oh, did it rain! Every man with a pail had to work hard and bail.

Sailor Taylor said, I think I should
just take the train.

Fun Facts About
Sailing  Ships

- People in Spain once made a huge model ship. It was more than 27 feet high. It was more than 42 feet long. And it was made *totally* of chocolate!

- The largest sailing ship ever built was the *France II*. It was more than 400 feet long. That's longer than a football field.

- Long ago, there were no maps to tell sailors where to go. They used the sky instead. In those days, sailors watched the sun. At night, they watched the stars.

- Joshua Slocum was the first person to sail around the world alone. He set out in 1895. He was at sea for three years and two months. He sailed 46,000 miles.

- Sebastian Clover was a sailor. He was the youngest person ever to sail across the Atlantic Ocean alone. He was 15 years old. He finished his journey in less than one month in January 2003.

You need to know the parts of a ship to sail a sailboat. Every part has a special name:

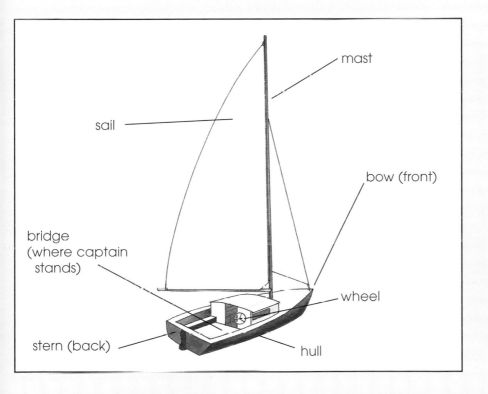

mast

sail

bow (front)

bridge
(where captain
stands)

wheel

stern (back)

hull

Build a Ship

You will need:

- 1/2-gallon milk or orange juice carton (wash it out)
- colored construction paper
- clay
- drinking straw
- tape
- markers
- safety scissors

1. Set the milk carton on its side. The spout should face down.

2. Cut pieces of construction paper. They should be the same size as the sides of the carton. Tape the paper to the carton. Use markers to decorate the sides of your boat.

3. Cut a triangle out of construction paper. One edge should be shorter than the drinking straw. Decorate the triangle. Use markers. This is your ship's sail.

4. Tape the edge of your sail to the straw. Press a piece of clay to the top of your boat. Stick the bottom of the straw into the clay. This is your ship's mast.

Word List

Challenging Words

bigger	Sailor
birthday	tailor

Decodable ai & ay Words

bail	paid	said	Thursday
bait	pail	sail	train
Cain	paint	Saturday	Tuesday
day	plain	say	wait
Friday	play	Spain	Wednesday
mail	rain	Sunday	
Monday	Ray	Taylor	

High-Frequency Words

a	get	my	they
all	go	no	thing
along	going	not	think
and	had	on	to
another	hard	our	too
back	has	please	us
bring	her	set	want
but	I	she	was
came	is	should	we
did	it	some	were
eat	just	soon	what
every	let	take	will
food	man	the	with
for	money	then	work
friend	must	there	you